T0077921

Sparkly Cakes & Cinnamon Swirls

stories & poems

BRENDEN HAUKOS

BALBOA.PRESS

A DIVISION OF HAY HOUSE

Balboa Press books may be ordered through booksellers or by contacting:

Balboa Press
A Division of Hay House
1663 Liberty Drive
Bloomington, IN 47403
www.balboapress.com
844-682-1282

Print information available on the last page.

ISBN: 978-1-9822-6616-5 (sc)
ISBN: 978-1-9822-6617-2 (e)

Balboa Press rev. date: 02/07/2023

Contents

May you be a Magical Mirror:
Whatever the world sends you,
May you always reflect back love~

This book is dedicated in admiration to Valentina Shevchenko.

Frog Spiritses

Let me tell you a story, dear listener. As we sit by the fire-side, I will listenly tell you. It means a dear lot to me.

I hope you like it, listener. But don't listen too closely please.

I wouldn't want to interrupt your daydreaming.

I love meeting you sparkly places, dear listener, in the realms of frog spirits. Well it's not really frog spiritses realms, but the frog spirits are there too.

I assure you, dear listener, they'll be buzzing for you.

Sparkly Cakes and Cinnamon Swirls

The Sparkle Fairy was getting sadder and sadder every day. All the cinnamon swirls she had stored for her friend the White Witch had grown stale over the days of his absence, and since the White Witch was not one to lie, especially to his bestest, the Sparkle Fairy if she had any hope left was now holding onto the frayed hem of it.

The nearby squirrels could sense her dismay, so they tried sitting still as they could, when they really wanted to race spirals up the trunks of birches and chitter in glee to the balmy spirits of the breeze this lovely time of spring.

"Keep the fire for us, dear," were the last words he'd said, on his way to the town, a week ago now. With a wink, he was gone. She had to smile at his stark *caw*, coming back to their clearing, from the edge of her hearing.

The fire dwindled desperate low, the wood he had split now ashes, and every twig lifted was a nightmare burden to her fragmenting heart.

The squirrels heard the sneeze and gasped in silence. The moss shuddered stiff under foot of a Coyote wandering this magical wood. And the tears the Sparkle Fairy sprayed unrecognized from her lips spelled doom for their convivial fire.

The scream -- it screamed the Sparkle Fairy for the very first time.

And blood took on new meaning in the veins of her mind.

The Coyote, in haunted fright, acted fast.

Now trapped deep in the den of the Coyote with no room to nudge and enough air to breathe, the Sparkle Fairy lay protected under spell of sleep. While she slept, she dreamt.

Once upon each early spring, the Friendly Flowers bloomed cinnamon swirls. There was enough sweetness there for all the frolicking fauna in the magical forest the Sparkle Fairy and the White Witch called home.

"I need to make a brief trip to town," the White Witch told her, while she was sniffing the hope-flowers. It was their day to collect cinnamon swirls, but she was okay to do it alone. *A brief trip.* "Keep the fire for us, dear..."

The Coyote had never thought highly of the dainty Sparkle Fairy or her flimsy friend the White Witch. Nor did he ever deign in times prior to converse with the crows.

Now there was weirdness rippling the air he breathed and a dark, dark and sharp, sharp scare haunting the edges of his frenetic gaze. He too was to make a trip to the town, though he knew not how *brief.*

And later that day, when he found like a stain smack on the ground the White Witch's White Hat blood-spangled and smashed, the Coyote's heart with a start knew a fear more intense than it could ever have imagined.

But when he found the beginning of the Spirit Card trail, his vision came back and his pace quickened.

The Coyote had never before felt respect for a man, especially the flimsy White Witch, always hiding away.

Back in the magical forest, amongst the fungi and ferns, the hope-flowers were singing anew.

The White Witch had dreamed, in purest horror, the scene of the Mace's making, and now he lay chained in that self-same chamber staring out of eyes almost sealed in bruises, and the Mace of Immanence stared violently back. He was down to one final Spirit Card, the last thread of Chance, but by any account he could realistically conceive, there was no help on the way, only a Cruel Executioner.

It is no matter how long it took, for when the Cruel Executioner arrived, leather-strapped and muscle-clad, the only words he had intent to utter were in the language of murderous Violence. The air around him bled black veins that seethed suppressed rage. He hefted the Mace of Immanence. The wood-lines were crawling like ant-hills; the gnarled barbs promised bitter gore.

The White Witch spat -- phlegm, blood, and grit. He strained his head upward and held the Cruel Executioner's eyes in his brave gaze. "You are responsible for what you do."

The Cruel Executioner responded: "I know."

With the last gasp of his magical strength, the White Witch sent his last-held Spirit Card -- "angelic protection and mercy" -- spinning across the stone floor and skirting under the door.

The Cruel Executioner paused in a moment of perplexion, looking back, and in that moment the Coyote burst through the doorway, launched himself at the Cruel Executioner, and tore with his canines into the man's throat. The Mace of Immanence fell in clanging echoes to the floor.

The way back to the magical forest was full of difficulty, and there was blood on the hands of the White Witch that needed cleaning. Thus they stopped off at the Wellspring of Life in the eastern wing of the forest and rinsed amongst the swirling tadpoles. A Blue Heron sailed by in the partly blue sky.

The White Witch and the Coyote brought the Mace of Immanence to the den of the Great Bear. They left it lying across the entrance. A low menacing rumble from below was all the trust they needed. They walked away with a slow, measured gait.

In her dreaming the Sparkle Fairy's tears had turned to streaming; her hope had burned as low as the guttering fire-licks. The dissonant song of crows stretched her sore mind to and fro when... gently... all of a sudden... the nightmare dissolved... and she found herself looking into familiar eyes and following the lines of a familiar voice:

"Let's go on bake some sparkly cakes, babe," the White Witch said.

Hummingbirds

The hummingbirds came out for the man, on in his days
The man came out for them, in the pale break o' day

To feed them, be with them, as always

A picture painted in time
— flitting, ecstatic, simple —
As was the man, birds brushing buzzingly against
— the chaparral fabric receding
In time —

The Mighty Oak

Will you go as the Mighty Oak goes, into the earth above and the sky below?

Will you know as the Mighty Oak knows, while the burble brook flows and the fierce wind blows?

What is lost when weakness shows, and what is told in the song of crows, when the stout heart beat of the Mighty Oak slows?

Frozen Verse

What's one more little landfill when that Landfill is me, sitting here rotting indefinitely? thought the planet the day she told the plants-and-such to turn the air off

What did the poor spirits of all those poor indefinitely rotting panthers lying there have to do with the giant Landfill I've become? she thought. Not much

She had endured a lot recently and it's not that it was the first or will be the last time but

All that ancient starlight often in their travels endured pains to avoid landing here for fear of getting lost and locked in a broken-hearted labyrinth designed by acute-and-skilled destitutes-of-spirit

Rapier

all my most important points
I thrust into
what must've been deaf ears

and these so-called men
must be bloodless cowards
as from what I thrust my sword point into
nothing came out

not even a squeak

Star Pig !!

If it wasn't for this whole global pandemic thing and all the fine American restaurants sitting around in limbo right now with everyone else, I would send you a hopefully-charming and certainly-respectful little note politely requesting a date with the awesome and lovely ** STAR PIG ** !! -- not for a romantic or even a tranquil evening, but just because we want to stick out our snouts for-the-heck-of-it where they may-or-may-not belong and really PTFO (pig the f*** out) on a pile of Chinese buffet. Dang that would be a lot of fun!

Just so I don't go too far without yet going far enough, and with the most accessible sweet spot sometimes proving very difficult to locate in the type of situations like this one that operates under the banner of Any Given Situation -- there's a lot of historical momentum behind other similarly-intended banners like Once Upon a Time...

As in, once upon a time, I met Star Pig !! at the Great Wall Buffet. We had fun pigging out, and we had even more fun pretending everything was sushi, and the only rule of that game that we bothered following was that before we took a bite of something new we had to look the other pig in the eye and tell him/her what kind of roll it was.

By way of example, I told the gorgeous Star Piggly-Wiggly, excuse me I mean Star Pig !!, that "Now I'm going to try the spread-out-breaded-chicken-bits-laquered-in-cheap-but-tasty-before-it-becomes-cloying-after-you-eat-too-much-but-not-enough-red-saucey-sauce roll" and she giggles at that and after maybe peeing her pants out of a brief but uncontrollable burst of pleasure despite the fact that neither of us were wearing pants, as pigs, but only shirts and shoes, the minimal requisite for service upon entry, and maybe this will strike you as a surprise but it was not even all the peeing and pooping we were doing while we were eating and play-pretending that was in fits and bursts making its way from our bodies, onto the chairs, and on down to the floor that ultimately represents the impetus that got us kicked out of that restaurant before we had finished eating ourselves to the point of absolute stupor, and all we really know about it is the affable Johnny scolding us on our way out that "It takes a real couple of pigs to joke around about Chinese food being Japanese food in a Chinese restaurant," but we were laughing all the way home thinking about how the affable Johnny had turned all red in the face and all black in the eye, and the thing that really kept us laughing even harder was the thought of Johnny being stuck cleaning up all the mess we had left -- the piss & the s*** -- literally everywhere and we didn't care much about having offended poor Johnny on that basis because we were a couple of pink American pigs that just wanted to get back to my trough, a sweet spot which was close enough to the sweet sweet spot where we were really going, because what we really wanted to do after all that fun will only be described as becoming one in that place in time, namely "a sushi roll in the hay", or even "two pigs in a blanket" ((again) of hay) and all the while not-much-caring about

Johnny's, anybody's, or our own history...but before we get any bit farther ahead of ourselves, let us remember that while at this point both myself and Star Pig !! are undoubtedly primed for the down-and-dirty getting that will soon get done, all the while in that instance generating a special secret that was just between Star Pig !! and I, and I am going to hint-hint try not to tell you.

We are in fact still sitting there in the poopy pee-piles on our chairs and playing a game whose first rule (look him/her in the eyes before eating) is meant more as a suggestion and whose only other rule (name the food after a sushi roll) is meant to be followed with a stringency without whose backing the game runs the risk of not being fun, and in case you the reader has forgotten after all this time, I just said "Now I am going to try the spread-out-breaded-chicken-bits-laquered-in-cheap-but-tasty-we'll-just-say-before-you-or-me-or-anyone-else-for-that-matter-eats-too-much-of-it-and-it-goes-from-being-tasty-to-(being)-cloying-saucey-sauce-sauce roll" and after giggling and peeing and before we got off track and eventually lived happily-ever-after the end.

Star Pig !! responded "Oh yeah, how is it?" and I responded "Pretty spread out" and she didn't giggle but said "Now I'm going to try the tantalizing-by-way-of-being-forbidden-yet-flavorful-cannabalistic-fried-egg-roll roll" and I exclaimed "Oh yeh?! That'll make a poop !!!!!"

And there are certainly others, but we'll stick with Any Given Situation in this given situation, thanks be to God for the giving and to the angels for their protection and mercy, and we're going to put a bow on this as follows: there's a little secret that I'm not supposed to tell you if for no other reason than that loose lips sink ships, but since I know I can trust you I am going to tell you: I called her War Pig back in that hay loft: it was supposed to be our sultry secret: she called me her four-star general: that stopped the sauce right then and there: "Only four stars?": "Well how many do you need, big boy?": "I need all of them": "Say it again. I like a man with ambitions": "I need all of them": "You'll be my Infinite Star Mercenary General. How do you like that?": "I like it a lot": and all that came next was a bunch of Eskimo-kissing, which pigs have a natural evolutionary knack for, it turns out, and the rest was history, maybe?

But all that being said, I should have never told you that secret. Now Star Pig !! will never trust my ability to keep a secret, she'll never fulfill my dream of her becoming War Pig, and therefore I'll never fulfill my dream of becoming the Infinite Star Mercenary General ISMG. I guess it's not going to happen now. Cat's out of the bag. And everybody knows that the pig who can take enough time off of social media these days to come up with a convincing strategy for snaring a cat, to say nothing of the miracle it would take for him to pull it off even if he got to the place where he would try, yes, we all know that's just some mythical pig, a distant hypothetical that humans hope they'll never have to rely upon for sustenance, no matter how scarce resources get before the world ends, and before the world ends, I starve to death, or that cat-out-of-the-bag does everything it could ever do outside of that bag in any universe known or un- while still maintaining certain ranges of fluctuation that allow it to be considered at least in one sense or another the same cat eventually gets bored of everything and crawls back into the bag and forces me to start rethinking and reconsidering the potential for that date once again after all...that roll in the hay...I'm going to call it a...dang she's pretty.

Such were the musings of a random pig, as he gazed for the first time at the lovely blue-and-pink visage of the indelible Star Pig !!

The City

I am like the city:
I want to fly high
like the birds.

I am like the city
stuck in one place
like a light
stuck on red.

Osprey

Osprey, only in flight
can I read your Name
in the upward lilt
of your outspread wing.

As you sit perched there,
Osprey — bleeding dread stain —
upon the air between us
all I can name
is death, is life,
is the thing.

Mad Hatter

I have somehow been usurped by the demonic visitation of
the Mad Hatter
and cannot shut up really please
and not even try really sneeze, until snoring pipe down a bit
out the blowholes of even-steven said me,
after apologies hard self-enclosed and unself-solated cries
just to give some shine to while sleeping dogs lie
over coffee, tv, solitaire, and all the other unlikes they never
really anymore really really liked
since yon moreover to let sleeping dogs sleep, and in sleep let
sleeping dogs dream, and in dream let dreaming dogs really
whine, and
lowercase i I tried,
"You white lied," you said snide.
I look you in the eye: those sleeping dogs in dreaming whine,
and we're gonna let em do it.
We're letting em let it all out, indulgent or not much that
they want period in any dream dreaming dog-like colonized
country somewhere,
and did I remember like I wanted to tell you earlier before I
finally get and here be a gaseous green blue and yes that was
purple it windbag to the point:
you better listen closely, cuz they protected you your whole
lives, you little snook-ems!
Would you like some crumpetcakes now!!?

I   brimming   bangladesh-led-sausage-flying-links-why-
pancakes-over-not-only-runny-eggs-orwhynoteven-#friedfr
ogribsforchangebreakfastyfast
but only in your quarters please
while we thru the wee wee hours and by unbinary nature
naturally need to unun-getup, liking tulips -- oh by the way,
my daughter's last name -- and unguiltfully wee,
but we here not saying please are not going to sit with our
wees in our hands all night.
I shouldn't have to say that to you, should I?
They make fireworks for that.
You need to get your Discrepancy Rating Interface Protocol
prognosticated before the flood or worse: you forget to
munch the twirlycakes.
I mean you did pay admission, right?
There must be a ticket floating the breeze somewhere around
here.

And even if there isn't for the most precise and only hard-
working man worth-his-salt kind of reason why you need
not apply knives more directly fly times or specifically unun-
getup again-gain for the not-un-not-gipper ungaining you
something, as in to rinse your hands
of whatever mote of dust migrated over grabbing your wee;
I will never be rude: make you wait in your head, hesitate
from the plate to the pate, and I'm in there sure you could fit
one more in your diggle-do stuffed noggin.

Aren't they sweet, you asshole?. Swallow, practice I'm sure, down digggle-do, before I already said you need to eat and have already paid for the crumpetcakes,
as verify over there the white hare can willing and willing can can do
cuckatoo-too-too rama-lama rama-lama ding-ding do
but will never ever, never ever do for you

and most especially obviously after you fish-fileted his we're not even going to
I'm sorry buddy now even after that time censored storybook written with a plot of land where I live and aside you white rabbit visiting did offend the morning glories with a wrong-rubbing non sequitur
go there.
But even if he won't tell you, I will right now, but for the sake of stopping because I can if I want to. The end. Goodnight.
Encore: of the details detailing detail-ridden squandered old-times already yesterday.
Yeesh! that was fast!
When needing to bake for you crumpetcakes decked in pink frosting and so smothered in white sparkly sprinkle-bits you would've just adored them,
if I hadn't first told you by way of a long getting introduction longer than you would have thought in our post-brunch jetlag syndromey thing-things,
but before I don't wait to saying say after how the end already came a long time ago now.
You must have forgot,

and even then already too late to have spent my whole life's savings on the first little white sparkly sprinkle-bit for you, and you don't even want to know 'bout the frosting O my dear and O dear don't ask why or how spent my whole life's savings on one little white sparkly sprinkle-bit for favoring you this eve,

while we wait as earl grey's gray gay host as in happy makes way for the coast as in at dawn,

as piper's delirium bells play,

as to the edge of his chair O said over there white hare creeps a little too close and by wayward way to remind that where I from somewhere come there one never there could find a chap who would not 'fore too long stuff food in my face for free just to see in my teeth feed, as I'm sure you could guess.

But not for me but for thee these white sparkly sprinkle-bits were,

so I took out a short-term loan, so then I could downpay a little-more lengthwise some may say longer-than-life type like loan,

but don't worry for me. The loan's in your name.

Don't be silly. Really, I forged the contract.

Good luck paying it!

Though surely worth it I'm sure you'd say if veritable brimming your lips weren't with crumby-thing-like overflow, and before earl grey gets here to kill the vibes,

and after chastise I remind you that I love you,

but did I leave anything out?

The blue pundits arguing are and in until face they're but there there they'll be okay someday.

And even if logic contend by now nothing have I left out logically, well it doesn't logic: it's more of a muscle memory thing, you see.

And really one more diggle-do would diggle-do you do well, sir.

Listen close. Open wide. I'm going to help you cram this last one in,

all the while I enjoy my impossible lollipop unwrapped with glee glee glee,

and don't look at me like that all bulging-eyed.

I, for one, have never practiced the heimleich manoeuver,

and I prolly need a break from all this gaseous gabbing and a breath, don't you think pretty sure sunshine...

Swans Silent Swam

Eleven swans silent swam
skirting the surface
of tranquil waters.

Below them teemed hundreds of tadpoles,
filtering through the suspended murk
and darting past lily pad stems.

From above, amidst the outcropping
of glossy green pads,
a flower's white benediction
inspired of the setting.

Nearby,
the swans had through
their lightness of touch
already fully submersed.

A Witch's Rattle

It was made simply
of a tincan of eaten blackbeans
neatly cleaned rinsed and dried.

Then filled a fifth up
with dried split pea,
and sealed off with
a cardboard lid and straps of black duct tape.

Most often it sat and waited for a proper time
to call out to its friend
so it could take her places.

The Magician

She was the Dancing Fox,
dancing away at World's End.

She was the Singing Crow,
singing the Song of World's End.

She was the Quietest Buffalo,
bearing Witness to World's End.

She was a Puff of Smoke.
Look, and she'll be gone.

The Fairy

I sat a pit with fairy friend
with wit
who spoke fine like fire-lines skyward
with his fingers and in the words
of forgetting
he uttered my name.

I will never remember why
and how
he came iridescent at day's fall
under unblemished sky
to a new frontier which was my own future-seeking heart.

I asked him his
but in the wilderness of his answering
gaze bracken-bound
and raven-traipsed
with machete for clearance still striking
and only now for what comes next.

Weeping Willow

Willow trees remember their tears in
strands of rustling green.

Willow trees keep their watery leaves
and cry them always a little more.

When you remember the trees -- the
mighty oak, the tender birch -- remember
the willow too with gratitude.

For it is she who remembers your
ancient grief.

Acrostic

Sometimes it all

Takes so much courage, and the

Rapport with oneself to know, and the

Energy to do what

Needs

Getting done

Today.

However, it ain't ever easy.

Miss S.

Dear Fair Missus
the hope-flowers sang silent songs of praise
the day I met you.

In truth, you are fairer
than any flower.

In truth high praise this be,
for most men and women
are no more than
skin-bags of toxic waste sustained
by a hint of grace.

While most flowers are angels
who tired of heaven
for the time being.

In another life,
when I am not quite I,
and you are not quite you,
I'd like to marry you.

Then we'll take tea together,
and share all the pretty sunsets.

Alas I'm certain I'll never really meet you
really.
And whosoever said life isn't tragedy?

Urban Tulips

That measure of grace
for a poet transfixed
by a vase of urban tulips
cannot except by grace be expressed.

Yellows, oranges, reds,
all popping bright,
and newly fallen across the tablecloth,
a lace-trimmed expanse cluttered
with cupped petals
like lil wrinkled boats,

as if a troupe of forest nymphs
were taking to the great
white sea beyond.

As for this poet transfixed:
the moment of grace
lived in his heart, yeh,
not his pen, that day--

from the momentary glimpse
to the long gaze that followed--

while morning sunbeams through yon window broke
and a chipmunk chittered wildly over his acorn treasure.

To Hathor

from the Eratospheres

Speak to me, O holy cow,
upon whose breast, and to whom,
I seek come haven home.

O Hathor O divine eternal O beauty herself personified O
love-giving life-to-us-all-lending O great goddess O one

My oh my and do I dare?

Do I dare, dear Hathor, beseech thee
in this my hour of unholy want:
Do come hither.

And on the rapturous cusp
within the veil of our mutual gaze
you will see me sincere. I am, and
I do love you, dear burning goddess.

To the core of you, I do implore you --
stooping low to this lowly man where he stands --
O Hathor, give me your hand!

Let us start with a touch.

Osiris Entombed

The virulence of a god
is nothing to be
trifled with, and

Osiris entombed
was not a happy
man.

It was from the places
of the most heinous intimacy
with his own god's soul
that the Curses issued forth,
spoke from the barbed-off
pit of his hatred.

He cursed Seth,
so-called brother,
to desecration, to torture,
to dismemberment —
being torn to fragments,
each useless piece of him
acutely and eternally aware
of its own torment —

But those Curses thus
uttered in a tomb,
had nowhere to go but

from Osiris's lips
to Osiris's ears.

When after extensive seeking,
Isis finally found the casket,
washed up in a mangrove thicket,

she shrieked
at what was left inside.

Life and Death in the Early Times of the Hill Country named Virtigia

First Chronicle

The first chronicle marks the clasping of hands and the naming of Virtigia. Mark One - Name Onnus.

44 hinds raised Thukar's hand. Errant Pale raised Strykos's hand. In combat, Strykos killed Thukar. Strykos raised 44 hinds' hands.

Errant Pale we fed to the pit of vipers.

Many hinds spat under the sun that day, but that night there were some chuckles around the fire-pits.

Strykos crossed legs with the Witch Enschantara on the platform in the Mighty Oak our Majesty. Meanwhile, we the hinds bled our knives.

Thus opened a night of flowers blossoming. Marked I, Onnus the Bloody.

Second Chronicle

The second chronicle in the early times of Virtigia as enscribed by Yep the 2nd chronicler, named First Scribe of Virtigia by Strykos the day the Law cut down Onnus the 1st chronicler. Strykos bled his own side that night. And that night wolves made a kill. Their howls resounded across the hill country.

In the mist of daybreak, the Witch Enschantara called for a day of feasting.

This came during the hour of her blessing hiddens geyser forth.

A blue jay pecked at kernels near the base of the Mighty Oak.

Strykos ascended to the platform in the heights of the Mighty Oak, bearing the Witch Enschantara in his arm. His kin known as Heppe followed him up the ladder. To bring the child forth into Virtigia.

Third Chronicle

The third chronicle tells of the beating black-and-blue of the girl named Fleur, who was the offspring of Strykos and the Witch Enschantara the night they locked legs after Virtigia was named. The 2ⁿᵈ Chronicle tells of Fleur's birth.

A fair hind though she was, Fleur subsisted as a Curse upon Virtigia -- and upon the mind of our leader Strykos.

It was in fact Strykos himself who beat the girl-hind with a dried strap of cedar brush.

This happened the day the youngster first took to her feet.

He beat her in a clearing, unwitnessed except of the sun overhead. He did it within an inch of her life.

To occupy the hinds meanwhile, the Witch Enschantara made Spirit Song on the slopes of the western hills while we all sat on the hill-side. She spoke spirits that day --the sad, the delicate, the violent, the remorseless -- too many altogether and the unnameable beside --

Strykos returned from the North carrying Fleur in his arms. His steel gray eyes showed sign of earlier tears. Upon handing over Fleur into the Witch Enschantara's care, he called forth Heppe. In front of all the hinds gathered before the Mighty Oak, Strykos embraced Heppe.

We all believed Strykos would bleed himself that night, but he did not.

Fourth Chronicle

The fourth chronicle tells of the arrival of bitter white water blankets to cover all the nearby hills and valleys. This terrible yet beautiful thing we called 'snow.' The snow came after days and days of blowing rains.

So that all could see, Strykos ascended the Mighty Oak to its highest heights. So that all could hear, Strykos exclaimed: "de Kaandi i'i wuu-vi'i." Then he let go and fell to the earth.

Covered in a coat of snow, Strykos gathered up and struck down the five weakest hinds in Virtigia: 4 boys, 1 girl. All, naturally, youngsters.

Then Strykos cawed many caws, like the crows, and he bled both his arms with his legendary sword.

A Black Night followed. Lovers huddled close in their huts. Not speaking.

In the morning, the bodies were burnt. The Witch Enschantara sang an Elegiac Hymn for each of the fallen five. The desolate wails of the mothers she strung into her nightmarish harmonies of such cathartic import. Her music came over us like ocean breakers on the rocks. Many tears were cried.

The third day after the snow-fall, it was a happier Time. Young hinds played War Games with the white snow. Laughter resonated across Virtigia once again.

That evening, Strykos demonstrated himself burrowing down into the snow. He re-emerged sometime later, got his two wives, and brought them down into the burrow with him. Many other lovers acted in the same element.

Fifth Chronicle

The fifth chronicle tells of the forming of the Conscript, a military unit comprised of all able-bodied man hinds of full build and whichsoever able-bodied woman hinds of full build as desired to join. In front of the 23 members of the Conscript -- 18 men, 5 women -- Strykos gave a stirring speech from the Mighty Oak. The Law saluted them three times with his sword.

The Witch Enschantara initiated each individual conscript in private, in her scrying chamber. From the moment of their initiation forward, each member of the Conscript was no longer to be known or addressed as 'hind.' Now they were all 'elders.'

Strykos and his inner circle were known at that Time to say: "Respect your elders."

The Conscript were given a fermented milk around the fire-pits that night. A barn owl presided over the merry-making from another nearby oak.

There was much laughter that night, but before dawn the Conscript were back on their feet and ready for War Games.

Sixth Chronicle

The sixth chronicle tells of the departure of a War Party. In past times, War Parties were selected once every moon cycle. They were selected of the hinds, and the selected War Party would surveil surrounding territories and hunt game to feed Virtigia for the coming moon. No two War Parties were ever the same.

When the weavers and the smiths had finished clothing and fitting with armor all the elders, the Conscript presented itself to Virtigia on the Eastern slopes. The Witch Enschantara sang Glory Tunes. We the rest of the hinds made note of the curious fact that the Conscript had presented itself in two distinct groups, standing apart a full five paces. Both groups had distinct uniforms, and both groups stood under a different banner.

When the Witch Enschantara had finished, and the crowd had finished its hoorays, Strykos spoke. He announced the latest War Party, which was to depart before daybreak. Then he announced the splitting of the Conscript into two factions -- the Clan of the Wolf, and the Clan of the Badger. Strykos himself, as leader to the Clan of the Wolf, would be leading his wolf brethren on the War Party.

The Clan of the Badger, with Darius as its leader, would be staying behind to guard over Virtigia. Handsome Darius spoke next. He swore loyalty to Strykos and his wolf compatriots. Then he swore loyalty to the hinds of Virtigia. Next he swore loyalty to his badger brethren. Lastly, he promised to protect Virtigia to the best of his abilities in the stead of our beloved Strykos.

Many words were uttered that night -- be they solemn, amorous, or otherwise -- between elders and their lovers. Tracts could be written of those conversations, had they not occurred under the obscurity of whispers in the privacy of huts.

By dawn, the Clan of the Wolf was gone.

Seventh Chronicle

The seventh chronicle tells of the trial of the thief Jopopo under the steady hand of the Law, who had the full backing of Strykos and Strykos's legendary sword.

Jopopo had stolen blankets from a tradesman's supplies. He had done this during the Time when the Clan of the Wolf was on War Party. The Clan had returned with a pair of cows and a bull too.

On the first day of his return, the Law had already informed Strykos of Jopopo's foul deed and the need for trial. The lines on Strykos's face seemed a shade starker than usual. He settled in for a few days, then called the trial together.

The Law punished Jopopo with a pair of matching tattoos -- a thick solid line around each wrist. These tattoos served as a promise that if he stole again, it was off with his hands.

After the Law announced the verdict, he released Jopopo so the thief might return to his hut.

Eighth Chronicle

Chronicle 8 tells of the arrival of Spring Fires and the melting of the White Water Blankets that had covered the Land through the turning of five moons.

When the Eastern Fields were green again, we held Dances for five days and five nights. The Witch Enschantara sang Spirit Choruses for us to dance to. All of our blood -- the men, the women -- it roiled like field-fires across the hills and valleys.

On the first night of Dances, the Law made an announcement. This announcement he proclaimed with the full backing of Strykos's legendary sword:

"I herby state that all members of the great community of Virtigia shall now be called 'men' or 'women.' No longer shall any man or woman be called 'hind.'. Members of the Conscript shall still be respectfully addressed as "elders."

After five days and five nights of Dances, we held two days of Feasting. On the second night, near the end of the feast, the Witch Enschantara held the very first Theatre of Spirit. Her pupil worked closely along side her to achieve this.

Daisies were budding in the Eastern Fields.

Ninth Chronicle

The ninth chronicle sets forth the Early Hill-Country Time when Eel Heppet spoke the Prophecy forth before a twilit gathering of men, women, and elders on a night when each person with one hand sat touching the soil and with the other hand touching another's hand.

When Eel Heppet had spoken the Prophecy forth, all of us peoples of Virtigia fell into line wandering past the Great Oak, and Strykos on each person's shoulder held a hand while each of us laid lips to the Upbraided Crow.

When our line had summated its wandering, Strykos let out a loud Moo in the nature of a bull, and then he in his lips tore the Upbraided Crow's neck from its wings and spat eyeballs.

Strykos is much loved of we his people, revered.

He and a Council of Three -- including the Witch Enschantara, Heppe, and the Law -- gathered in the Witch's hut and discussed until Day's Fall.

Tenth Chronicle

The Prophecy

"there will come a Time
when the raging roaring buzz of Flies
and before that Swarm itself consumes
but long after the Bull's last dance is spent
and long after any man's last breath
the music of the Hill Country of Virtigia
will be drowned in pestilence"
-- this Eel Heppet spoke forth

A Fragment of *Enschantara's Cosmogony*

as pilfered by chronicler Yep during the times of their wandering

The First God is the Everlasting Waterfall, the principle of transparence itself -- but not uniform like the air or aether... but like a liquid, all so sparsed in its falling flow that it gave rise to the Lesser Gods by making space for them.

The Second God is the Ray of Radiant Light...

The Third God is the Air Lord Arisen...

Fourteenth Chronicle

(the Eleventh through Thirteenth Chronicles are considered lost)

Chronicle 14 betrays:

At night at our gathering of Virtigians,
Strykos unsheathed his legendary sword
and struck down the weak-wristed weaver
who had stood and spoke against him:
Horoi the weaver fell
but half the gathered elders there booed and lowed.

Fragments from the *Journal of Yep* during the times of their wandering

Strykos: "All those Badgers are nothing more than fools! Do you see the things we've seen thus far, my friend Yep? The minerals, the oases, the plants, the trees, the fruit, the game -- all of it. And more, my friend. So much more. Those fools just sit there and starve, right next to a pit of vipers."

Strykos: "Wait…stop…look!"

[...]

Strykos: "He wants your flesh. You must scare him with the sign of magic."

Me: "The sign of magic?"

Strykos: "You must have one somewhere in that scribe's head of yours!"

Me: "Can you show me?"

Strykos: "If I show you, the lion will see that I am your master. Then he will most certainly devour you while I am looking elsewhere. Just make it work!"

Elegy for a Life in Lonely Places

It has drifted all the way down
the lonely mythical thing
born of dark's darkest wish
for a witness
here in the Ocean's deepest depths
where no stars ever shine

It has drifted all the way down
in death, to that tectonic shelf
upon which its bones now etch
the primeval script of loneliness

It has drifted all the way down
from unknowing witness of solitary life
to knowing unwitness of boundless death
in conjunct with the Ever
whose Pain now reads Poetic
among the fish-shaped skeletal forms
lying there

Drift down, O abyss, we cry --
you wore thin in the guise of a fish

Drift down, O mother of night, we cry --
your Conscript has settled on a surface

Drifted down now,
the names he spells are soundless utterances,
the letters he writes are shapeless forms

We cannot grieve for you, we cry --
We cannot grieve
We cannot

The Wild Blue Yonder

You'll never know
the way
if you're counting horizons
to get there.

You'll never really arrive
if you give the place
its name.

The Wild Blue Yonder
is the impossible sky
in which I aspire to fly.

I'll never blame you
for not trying.
But if try you will,
will you have this dance?
Pretty please.

For the efflorescences and the snowclusterflakes...

any memory that is worth its salt will train from the moment of its conception in whatever primordial womb somewhere until the moment of its birth in the heart-and-mind of whatever happenstance human happened to be there that day for each other and it arrives for the express purpose of uniting the novel present with its ancient roots

and natural-like it lived on in whatever happenstance human this one guy happened to be from that day on until he died whatever happenstance day

he died on

and that day it was you might say set free

the very idea of which does seem to live on with it as in a nagging itch why? all the time it spent wandering the landscapes of this one unimportant man's tenuous and gorgeous soul all those days and all those years later and it is not in the nature of an idea to measure and to weigh the fort and the heft of another man's time

all those things it met there were the friends it made and how they grew together

how those precious memories of the times when after shifting plates underfoot settled and while sleeping dogs still lie and in

the crisp perhaps air emergent feelings called forth this thing
once an idea made memory met with the very real fact of its very
real roots and its very real wings and the passing haze of its very
real dreams and its heart yes now it has one -- it prefers to nest
in a bed of moss and on ember-embossed bitter cold long stark
dark dark nights after musing over frost's filigree scripting that
always brought it back to the ununendings of the dark dark and
the night when it would buckle its boots bid again 'o the crows
and it in the guise of a guy by way of the wood set forth for the
town whatever happenstance man lived in

and innocuous as friends in the golden light of all of each
prior meeting

O how mortal days they fade into eventual obscurity where
what we won't go there awaits us but not for today
as always grateful patient working to be ever kind

and over coffee or tea, this guy really loved herbs, one of a
kind we appeared to any unnoticed passerby just any two
guys catching up over coffee reminiscing over the details of
the day or any day really looking back from this day before
it winds down to the bare nub where raw our hearts wait at
the edge of long-broken goodbyes

become dust you say, we'll do this another day

and we do, but not always forever, and at that point while we
are scribbling senseless words in the air for once again only
to say I love you man, I love you bro

it is always good to see you

but even though all the wishes in the world were there to see us that day, not a single one could make us stay, except just one extra moment beyond what was physically possible, at least at that time, and even that moment came and went so fast maybe no one ever even saw it happen and even if they did they would probably never guess that all that is precious in any universe anywhere resides in that one specific moment made from a wish that blustery day in whatever town two regular things in the guises of men sat at a table making friendship over coffee you'd think or tea maybe this guy really loved herbs heck if there was a passerby there that day who could have happened to notice something unsettle and someone asked her then by chance "guess what" she may have settled on "chicken butt!" if she was a young girl but not in a million years gone by would've guessed what really happened the day the universe was saved from things like meaninglessness and other nonsensical such truck as couldn't fit in the mind of a child but you'd think she must have felt it, something, maybe, like wonder like when we were also only youngsters

and one time really was the last last time really, sadly

the sky cold tears it cried that very real day

and the thing that was only just an idea before it met some such happenstance guy, and after all is said and done, at the end of the day, only just an idea once again once again upon a time there was a very bright idea, and none of the other ideas had any idea how come this idea could shine so bright, as small and simple as it has always been, yet if they knew in any way shape or form hidden inside this idea lived a human heart beating, they might have been able to bet that was it, that was the thing

but any safe wager would probably say that none of those diddly ideas could know squat about how in the haven of that human heart hidden under moss and frost lived the memories this little memory had of a man he really loved once upon a time, such a long time ago

or how in those treasured memories he could see his spotless self reflected and framed in stout oak as in a gentle tender mirror moving and what it's like to learn what it's like to be known through and through by a man that you love and in his terms loves you

and on

it is always nice to see you man. how have you been? what's new?

oh nothing really. good to see you. it always feels like it has been too long.

this guy really loved herbs

Brain Fart: A Virtigia Story

On an ancient battlefield, a brain fart will spell your doom, Darius: breathes the Witch Enschantara.

There was enmity here, in the Hills, and from the western slopes Strykos did Stare at the men of the Clan of the Badger.

Strykos had spoken to each of his eight warriors separately. "The Clan of the Badger are men, like you and me. They are starving, while you and me are fed of the wild fruits and the wild game of all this land. These men sit with their fingers up their hinds and wait for berries to grow, while we wander the wild woods and swim in the wild seas. The Clan of the Badger are no match for us. Be on your guard, and bring them to their knees."

"DEATH," resounded in the echoing hill country as Strykos and the Clan of the Wolf charged uphill fearlessly at the Clan of the Badger. Strykos did Roar.

It was something in the distance, a moment of distraction, that was the fatal step for Darius, their leader. They met in a scree of rock, and the slight trip led into the Legendary Saber of Strykos straight through the center of his spine and out his Solar region.

Strykos lost two men that Summer day.

For Our Memory:

Aedix Qua

Jor-rin

Ode to the Fighting Spirit

deep earth magic

Okay, I'm going to go somewhere and if you read along I'll do my best to make sure my directions give you the best possible chance to get here, granting that it is your ultimate responsibility to get here for yourself. Finally I will say by way of word of warning this: if you want to go, go; if you want to stay, stay. Follow these words into the wild wood world where we bleed me for you across hooked strings of loving light.

Either way, don't just write me a rain check on this one. You might think you'll come back at the right time later, and no one could legitimately argue otherwise. But -- you know it, I know it -- there have been a lot of rain checks written recently.

Armed with the common sense the good God gave us, everyone can agree that if enough mystical value could be injected into the idea of Common Sense, a good old-fashioned thing, then Common Sense would say the outlook on the value of rain checks is dismal.

Let's say you are a well-meaning person, and you went to the Common Sense Interface and asked why (specifically speaking: "why is the outlook on rain checks dismal?"). You are well-meaning because you were operating vaguely under a couple of assumptions -- namely that 1. common sense is good, as an idea this is very logically true -- at least up to a point, and maybe after, and if it were to become even untrue logically somehow sometime somewhere even if in any way only kind of, after all that the odds are still always good that it will go back to being true logically eventually, or so it seems to a human like me...and 2. the question "why?" is so satisfactorily compelling to me in its potential as a response to whatever the Common Sense Interface answered to my previous question just now.

In real-time, humans negotiate compelling ideas with magical solutions. Your magical solution, in this instance of 'let's just say', was to ask the question why. We'll call you Jumping Jehosaphat.

As for you and me, neither of us ever to my knowledge found the Common Sense Interface.

The CSI is basically an oracle, and yes in the old-time sense. And in the name of trying to clarify, let's just pretend that I am I and you are (just to pretend) the CSI, and I come to you to ask you a question...and here's the real distinction: whatever I ask you, if and when you answer me, that answer and the knowledge it reveals is not merely between me and you but becomes common sense in the common sense sense of the term, and goes on to operate on global types of scales. But moving on I will once again let you go on being you, perhaps enjoying a little wilderness exploration, and I of course will continue to be me.

Yes it is an oracle, and as such if a man has brought one question to the CSI he's already asked way too much according to the overwhelming majority of people's standards of living. One has got to imagine that at times in history specific discoverers of the CSI have sorely inflated the value of everyday common sense by severely overindulging their curiosities, and certainly social sparks flew around the world, and all just because they could.

But before we abandon all feeling for poor Jumping Jehosaphat to the scrap-heap of bad impressions, let me for more than just the sake of saying say: despite his recent cosmic blunder, Jumping Jehosaphat has a lot of real upward potential.

Jumping Jehosaphat did something I think will surprise you. Jumping Jehosaphat fasted on water for three days. Sitting still as he could, Jumping Jehosaphat gently observed a medium-sized boulder those three consecutive days just to see if he could sense the presence of thought within the stone.

This whole time he was also trying to engage the rock in mental dialogue or some kind of psychic interchange. Even a mere intuition. It takes a certain mad bent of rigorous spirit to go through with something like that, and I wanted to praise him for it if for no more reason than that he endured great pains and endured great pains gracefully, and he made great sacrifices, and he made great sacrifices for the reason all great accomplishments have ever been accomplished, specifically that he had nothing better to do, and just for the heck of it, and last and not least he did it in the true spirit of listening.

Without that listening spirit, the spirit of listening, which strengthens and emboldens our minds, even the smallest units of knowledge would not only be too heavy to lift but impossibly immovable burdens. And in the blind wanderings of our lives we would randomly and repeatedly stumble over invisible obstacles.

Now the interactions of what in this model are 'humans' and these what would appear to them as 'mysterious hindrances' have the awkward potential to model something for us.

I know this cliffhanger moment may-or-may-not have lost me some short-term trust, and I'm not going to be making any promises right now, but I will do this for you.

We're sitting around at a campsite picnic table somewhere up in the Colorado Rockies outside a little tourist town called Steamboat Springs. Tomorrow we will head into town and hit up the swimming pool. But we're not ready to crawl into our tents yet, and as we both remember, I told you I was going to do something for you. Yes I am going to give you something, namely an option.

This option I will thus make available unto your person; how I shall now tell you.

I'm not going to extend any more than minimal details in your direction, but I'll tell you this: I am going to leave an 'object' at the campsite, nearby the table. In hope I'll never know whether you take that 'object' somewhere with you from that day, but a safe bet says if you don't take it someone else soon will. I for one and for myself relinquish all claims of ownership in all or in part and parcel of this 'object'. I disavow all stake in whether you take or leave the 'object', and therefore I offer to you out of respect on my honor and to the best of my ability with full intention, both stated and not-, to maintain this sacred line in the sand and never to encroach upon the territories that proliferate forth from this option. The only thing I ask of you in return is that you freely and soberly consider the option to maintain, with integrity and sanctity, a sacred hidden space within your territories and leave a hidden trail marked for me in the liminal lands between mine and yours, not so much so that I would ever use it but except I could in the one most extreme of exceptional yet always potential cases, as a place of sojourn, if after having severed all ties fully and completely from this 'object', the result of which is the dissolution of the world of fellowship in which I live my life-per-say so that it becomes for all of us there a living hell. I ask this of you in the name of the reciprocal nature of the divine law of friendship. If you do set forth with this undertaking, I would suggest you beset my path to the hidden sanctum with the kind of high-stakes at-risk skin-in-the-game challenges without which life-per-say becomes unworth living some days. I left the 'object' as an option for you. God's graces unto us both if you don't take it.

Another bit back farther again now.

We got you lost off the trail, but I think with a bit of intented wandering we just might be able to get you back on the path back to the point which is the place and the camp we shall make and then break come dawn, and as you know I am already here, waiting to see what it all means when you arrive, hopefully not too late.

As a friend I am compelled to warn you, if this doesn't work out you're in for a long cold night, and I sincerely don't know how I could ever make that up to you. At that hypothetical point, had we any desire left to salvage the friendship we would have to negotiate at least one sincere apology contract ASAP in the form of a hopefully in-the-flesh exchange of especially words also gestures looks and on. Then we'd have to invest jointly in a venture in the meaning-values of forgiveness, and all the while walk on a certain degree of egg-shells with one-another, until at some point somewhere some amount of time later suddenly you and I are talking about how awful it was for you to spend that whole cold night lost up in the mountains shivering for eight straight hours and moving haphazardly and with tremendous discomfort into ever more contorted self-absorbing stiff forms, all the while lying unlevel on twiggy ground, and it wasn't the twigs gnawing at every inch of you that was really getting you, it was the fact that you were at the very end of your wits every time you thought you heard the sound of perchance a panther come to maim kill and eat you. You'd twist and turn look around and see nothing.

Maybe at that point you had to really overthink the dawn and no matter how painfully far away it still was for you it was still going to arrive, eventually. No judgement here, but you were probably running dangerously bat-s*** close to running out of the strength to survive. You took a modicum of solace when you needed it, where you could find it.

But somewhere between the lines of us sitting there rehashing the known details you suddenly see the humor in it, I guess, for perchance the very first time. By way of something in the nature of in human life how one thing inevitably leads to another, and to make a long story short: you laugh first, but we both get going both quick and good, and for awhile there it is so funny we just continue to laugh harder and harder together, and at that point before it all dissipates into the wonder of what was really so funny in the first place, we'll mutually know in each his own terms that the wound has healed organically.

But please calm down. I know that you feel I am wasting all this especially time and especially energy on hypotheticals when the whole system for us by many excellent standards of predictive measurement very well could-be and no-less probably is approaching a threshold of fatigue beyond which point passes the possibility to go on and continue, at the very least until morning. And all the while jabbering I appear to be, while you definitely are the one with skin in this game.

But before this boiling point basically-reached boils over farther, I would really like to remind you for the first time actually and how could I forget but before the panic gets any worse and thus after you've taken a few conscious breaths I would really again like to remind you dare-I-say for the first time that my sincere suggestion this precise present instance and with all encouragement I do now implore you: please stop, get a grip on your surroundings and look around, specifically up.

"Holy s***," you yelled out, surging back suddenly stumbling falling, looking up. A figure out of nowhere now standing in front of you -- and meanwhile you looking in part like wanting to fight and in part like wanting to plea, and also like you couldn't fully commit to either approach and -- it must have been him whose eyes you had seen that had startled you so, unattached as they had been to any body up there in the heights of that tree but only encased in murky darkness and looking down on you from an inplaceable place instilled with presence, aware.

As you had started stumbled and scrabbled back, he descended, and face-to-face both to your feet you both came. He was talking to you and trying to talk to you man to man:

"Now hold on; hold your horses there buddy. Don't try anything you're going to regret later. I'm not here to hurt you; I'm here to help.

"On top of that I have a question to ask you. If you can hear me, clearly understand me, then tell me: yes or no. Can I ask you a question, buddy?" By that point he'd found confidence to extend his hand and, securing a firm knowing grip into your shoulder, really begin to speak to you.

You struggled but managed to say yes.

The man said: "Listen close. Earlier you were thinking about how people don't know things. And you were even thinking that even though people don't know things, those things are still there, and they get in people's way without people being able to understand what's holding them back. Do you happen to remember any of that?"

"Yeh... kind of...," you said, and here the rumpled recesses of your ragged voice spoken softly sifted down into obscurity while the parts of the words that came out came across almost as croaks. "... ... but how did you know?"

The man said: "Hold on with that just a minute: there's more. You were thinking over all that and then you came to a cliffhanger moment. You meant to take a breather then get right back to the point you were making about something being able to model something, and you were about to explain it but you got off track. Remember that, don't ye?"

"Yeh."

"Can I be frank with you?" his voice came out in a long drawn friendly drawl, tinged with concern.

"You can say anything you want. You just saved my life."

The man said: "You were thinking so hard I could hear you from halfway across the galaxy. I am a compassionate man, and it hurt me to think how much pain you were in."

"What were you doing halfway across the galaxy?"

The man said: "I like jumping."

"You were jumping halfway across the galaxy!?"

The man said: "I've gotten pretty good at it over the years. They don't call me Jumping Jehosaphat for nothing. To be honest, I had the gumption for a bit more on that one, but I couldn't bear the thought of you spending the night alone without food or a fire, and on top of that stark raving mad. So I bailed on that jump and dropped in here. I'm sure there'll be another one later."

"Thank you so much."

Jumping Jehosaphat said: "Don't thank me yet. Now I don't know where you were going about that whole thing about this modeling that, but I do have some sense of where you were trying to get. Yes I do know that the first place you set out to get is now long-forgotten lore, but I'm also aware that early in your journey you sought a new destination. In fact, it was the way that second destination beckoned from out the blue that even caused you to forget where you were going in the first place. The bad part in all of this is that in setting forth for the second spot you somehow... somehow you staked the heart of a child in all of this."

The man went on: "I'm not saying you tried to do it. I'm not saying you didn't. I am telling you that you are responsible for righting that wrong. Even if the first try is a failure - you and I both know that failure could very well predicate future paths so that others might not suffer the same sad fate."

Jumping Jehosaphat went on: "I'm going to give you two choices. You can either start in with the modeling thing...or you can skip that thread and start right after. It's up to you. But we're not going to sleep till that kid gets some rest. Got it? It's only right."

"I was trying to think about a rudimentary scenario of the interplay of incommensurables where there are only two elements but both are legion and each instance of both the elements can be said to be autonomous -- and I wanted to extend this idea to explore some of the surrounding territory and how in not-knowing and learning how to navigate around such mysterious hindrances and that maybe in reality it was alternately their destiny to attain the strength to and gather these things."

Jumping Jehosaphat said: "And then what?"

"I was going to start the story, before I lost my way trying to introduce it."

"Yeesh."

You said: "Yeah, and to be honest I'm so exhausted I couldn't possibly begin to do it justice. So I'm going to concede. I'm not going to make it to that legendary start line today."

Jumping Jehosaphat said: "Don't give up now. "

You said: "Every time I set out to go somewhere I got distracted and lost along the way. Over time this has caught up with me and now all I'm left with in the trivial, mundane details of a really arid world is this one image. I'll tell you about it.

"The image is of a relatively impossible thing, but we can call it a human being, because in a lot of ways it looks and acts like one. Anyway this guy is born with one goal in his mind and one desire in his heart, and these two things happen to be one and the same, but maybe it's because this guy is operating in a somewhat overly complex universe that for him to try to sustain something so arcane…

"…and complicated as having both a heart and a mind, two different things, and the heart desiring and the mind pelting after a definable goal…

"Let's just put it straight… this poor thing was f***ed from the start. At the moment of his birth he knew in his mind that he was born for a purpose: to compete in a footrace…"

Jumping Jehosaphat exclaimed: "Alright brother!"

You continued: "…a footrace some specific place at such and such a time…"

"The second he was born it was off to the races, and he ran his heart out trying to get there…literally. He spent his entire existence running, knowing full well the futility of his efforts but also knowing that if he didn't give the totality of himself to fulfilling the only wish that could fulfill him, then he would not only die a failure by default, but he would be a greater and more deplorable failure for not even trying…"

"Naturally."

"And while he may-or-may-not have been able to win the race, he would be able to compete with other great likeminded runners. He might even have had a chance to make an indelible impression in the passing eyes of a woman there to witness the event."

"I like it."

"But all of this really runs the risk of being cast as a moot point, for the precise reason that even despite the fact that participation in this particular footrace was the only activity that was ever going to give his existence fulfillment...

"Because he was born to compete in this event, but something somewhere went haywire in the cruel hands of fate, and while this guy was born before the event took place but given the particularities of timing and specialization, even if he jumped up that very moment and ran as fast as he could sustain for as long as he could sustain it, even scaling barriers and crossing thresholds of endurance and perchance even finding things like second winds along the way and breaking records as to how fast one thing can travel from one place to another without breaking those records by so great a margin that it would destroy his own system...but even if he were to approach speeds of running that were so fast they almost destroyed the system and himself with it..."

Jumping Jehosaphat interjected: "Got it, brother!"

You went on: "... but didn't quite do so, even then he would never make it to this race on time, such a mythical creature is he."

You went on: "To have been dealt the ultimate insult by the hands of fate. There must be a reason somewhere, but haven't you learned yet when not to ask 'why?'"

Tearing up, you said: "The thing is, hero that this guy is, he didn't even hesitate.

"Over the course of his life," you said, "sometimes he ran faster and sometimes he ran slower, because he had no other choice, and at times he would catch second winds… and yes, sometimes he broke records. In the end, it didn't matter.

"The thing ran itself out. But it never gave up. At the very same moment the gun went off and the footrace began, that self-same Time, he turned the corner beyond a final threshold's fatigue, and his heart exploded.

"The moment of his death and the moment the footrace began are the Same moment.

"Some say he came within a few miles of the starting line and even heard the gun go off."

Jumping Jehosaphat slouched over his knees, wetter eyes than before.

"I will say this, and then I will wrap it up. To be honest, this isn't exactly where I thought I would end up, but now that I'm here I could think of no better tract to pitch a tent for the night and no better time to kick off my boots and put my feet up by the fire and no better company to keep the demons at bay."

"Same to you, brother."

"In the end, I'm going to try to pass this off as an ode to the fighting spirit. Seems like a stretch to call it anything at all after everywhere I've gone…perchance mad or down the spiral-paths of *chaos*, but I like odes to the fighting spirit. So I'm going to call it one.

"The fighting spirit is that mythical thing that goes down fighting. That's what it's here for."

Spirits Swirling

Since it's too late to be yesterday,
I'll live with the mixing colors of today.

Since it's too late to be yesterday,
I'll live in the mixing colors of today.

Since every color mixing is an angel,
May the bright healing light wash you through~

Spingle and Span

The White Witch was, at times, an excellent storyteller. One night, as they sat beside the fire, the Sparkle Fairy said: "Tell me a story, love."

The White Witch took a sip of brew and began: "Once upon a time, there were a pair of twins boys born to a family of merchants. They were identical in every way. Their names were Spingle and Span.

"One summer when they were still too young to remember, the plague came to town, and their parents sadly died. Spingle and Span were orphaned to two separate households: Spingle to a family of poor farmers and Span to a skilled crafter of trinkets.

"Spingle had to work hard every day of his childhood, and he eventually grew to be a strong man. In the evenings of his childhood, he liked to wander the countryside. One day he came upon a stream that was magical indeed. Whoever gazed upon this stream saw in his reflection the most beautiful face staring back at him. Though he was poor, Spingle saw himself as being more beautiful than anyone else he ever beheld, and over time, his pride grew and grew.

"On the other hand, Span lived in a kaleidoscopic household surrounded by the inventions of a great, but evil, imagination. In this household was a magical mirror, and he who gazed upon it saw only ugliness. Span learned many things from his crafty father, but inside he was bitter about his looks, which he thought were so unfair.

"Time spiraled on, and one day when they were both adults, Spingle and Span crossed paths in the streets of the town. Neither one recognized himself in the other, neither one could see the other as his brother, but something about the look of Span's face captivated Spingle.

"What are you staring at, you hideous thing?" Span, who was always uncomfortable being looked upon, said to Spingle.

Spingle, vain in the extreme, took great offense at this. A mortal brawl ensued between the two unknowing brothers."

"Oh no!" the Sparkle Fairy said. "What happened then?"

"Strong as Spingle was, and crafty as Span was, both suffered lethal injuries in the fight."

"They both died?"

"Yes."

"But that's so sad. Can't you tell me a happy story?"

"Not all stories have happy endings, my dear."

"I want a happy story," the Sparkle Fairy insisted.

"Did I ever tell you about the time the White Witch met the Sparkle Fairy?"

"No, no you didn't. What happened?"

"They lived happily ever after…"

The End

one apt last time for sakes and songs gone by
in blue memories receding
between the obscure dark of this room and
us lying here listening to preordained silences spoken
breathing out

THE END

Printed in the United States
by Baker & Taylor Publisher Services